"Reach for the stars!"
—Lucy

Library of Congress Control Number 2014947581
ISBN 978-1-62157-258-9

Published in the United States by
Little Patriot Press
An imprint of Regnery Publishing
A Salem Communications Company
300 New Jersey Ave NW
Washington, DC 20001
www.RegneryKids.com
www.Peanuts.com

Manufactured in the United States of America
10 9 8 7 6 5 4 3 2 1

Books are available in quantity for promotional or premium use. For information
on discounts and terms, please visit our website: www.Regnery.com.

Distributed to the trade by
Perseus Distribution
250 West 57th Street
New York, NY 10107

Where Did You Go, Charlie Brown?

Peanuts created by Charles M. Schulz

Written by Diane Lindsey Reeves and Cheryl Shaw Barnes

Illustrated by Tom Brannon

Little Patriot Press

School was out and the sun was shining.
Too bad there was nothing fun to do.

Ho hum. Days like this were good for Lucy's business.

The doctor is in!

Franklin was bored.

Linus was bored of being bored.

Sally wasn't so sure Lucy's advice was worth a nickel.

Lucy changed her tune when Schroeder stopped by.

She was getting grumpy by the time Marcie and
Peppermint Patty showed up.

"Hey, what about me?" Charlie Brown asked.

Lucy had a fistful of nickels, and she was ready for a shopping spree.

Everyone was confused about Lucy's rather unusual advice. Leave it to Linus to smooth things over.

"One person's insult is another person's inspiration," he said. "I say we turn Lucy's advice into adventures!"

"Are we having one of those when-life-gives-you-lemons-make-lemonade moments?" Peppermint Patty asked Marcie.

Take a hike?

Why not?

Franklin called out to Pigpen, "Let's pretend to be famous explorers. You be Lewis. I'll be Clark."

"Sure," agreed Pigpen. He had learned a lot about the
Lewis and Clark expedition in school. This was going to be fun!

By the time Franklin and Pigpen reached the top of the hill, Pigpen was complaining about his aching feet.

But he got no sympathy from Franklin. The real Lewis and Clark traveled nearly 8,000 miles across rugged terrain and raging rivers.

What was a little hill compared to that?

Whatever floats your boat?

It worked for Christopher Columbus. Let's give it a try!

"Did you know that Columbus found the
New World by accident?" Linus asked.
"He was on his way to India but got lost."

"That's what happens when you sail off from
Spain without a map," Sally explained.

Go jump in a lake?

How about swimming across instead?

"Did you know that Gertrude Ederle was the first woman to swim all the way from France to England?" said Sally. "She swam over 21 miles across the English Channel and broke a world record in swimming."

"Wow, that's impressive," Linus answered. "I just hope Snoopy makes it all the way across this pond."

Make like a plane and fly away?

Huh? "Who does Lucy think we are?" asked
Peppermint Patty. "Amelia Earhart?"

Not that it would be a bad thing if Lucy did think that.
After all, Amelia Earhart was the first woman pilot to
fly solo across the Atlantic Ocean.

Reach for the stars?

Why not shoot for the moon instead?

"This one is for you, Neil Armstrong, the first man on the moon!" Schroeder announced.

Then the sounds of Beethoven's *Moonlight* Sonata
filled the air.

The next day, everyone got together.

"What did you do?" "Where did you go?"
They all started talking at once.

I TOOK A HIKE LIKE LEWIS AND CLARK!

"Hey!" Lucy demanded.
"What are you talking about?"

"We took your advice," said Linus,
"and had the best day ever!"

"You're kidding, right?" Lucy was surprised.
This was not the outcome she had expected.

On second thought…

"My advice is worth more than this," Lucy said.
"It's time for a raise."

"There you are, Charlie Brown!" Linus exclaimed.
"Where have you been?"

"Where did you go, Charlie Brown?"
Everyone wanted to know.

"I got lost," Charlie Brown looked down at his shoes.
"Just like Lucy told me."

Lucy rolled her eyes. "What a blockhead!"

"Good grief," Charlie Brown sighed.

Where Did You Go?

Charlie Brown and his friends had some great adventures. Along the way, they were inspired by some famous explorers. They want to share their discoveries with you.

Where Did You Go, Franklin?

On an expedition like Lewis and Clark!

"Ocian in view! O! the joy!"
—Captain William Clark, when they finally
neared the Pacific Ocean

(Good thing Clark was a better explorer than he was a speller!)

I WANT TO GO CAMPING LIKE LEWIS AND CLARK!

President Thomas Jefferson commissioned Meriwether Lewis and William Clark to explore the Western part of the continent to find a waterway to the Pacific Ocean. There were only two problems: no one knew how to get there, and no one knew what they'd find along the way. Now that's what I call an adventure!

Lewis and Clark assembled a team, called it the Corps of Discovery, and set off to explore in 1804. They spent the next two years making their way all the way from Illinois to the Pacific. Before they were finished, they had traveled almost 8,000 miles by canoe, horseback, and foot. They discovered 300 new species of plants and animals and encountered nearly 50 Indian tribes during the journey. Future explorers and early settlers were especially grateful for the 140 maps Clark drew of their route!

Where Did You Go, Linus?

On a voyage with three ships like Christopher Columbus!

"By prevailing over all obstacles and distractions, one may unfailingly arrive at his chosen goal or destination."
—Christopher Columbus

Christopher Columbus sailed west from Spain hoping to find India in the East. When he arrived at one of the Caribbean islands we now call the Bahamas, he thought he had arrived in India. That's why he called the natives Indians. Are you following all this?

WHAT IF COLUMBUS HAD BEEN WRONG AND THE EARTH WAS ACTUALLY FLAT?

It is a little confusing, but it makes sense when you understand that Columbus believed the world was shaped like a pear. If that was true, he could head west, circle the globe, and end up back where he started. Columbus had to have a lot of courage to do what he did. He did what other sailors and explorers had been too scared to do. Back then, no one had ever sailed so far away from land before.

Columbus discovered that the world is rounder and much bigger than he had expected. He wasn't the first person to "discover" the Americas (after all, native people already lived there), but he did discover a New World and changed the course of human history.

TELL ME NO AND
IT JUST MAKES ME
WANT TO GO.

Where Did You Go, Sally?

Breaking world records with Gertrude Ederle!

"People said women couldn't swim the Channel, but I proved they could."

—Gertrude Ederle

By the time Gertrude Ederle decided to swim across the English Channel, she had already broken 29 national and world records in swimming. She had already won one gold and two bronze medals in the 1924 Olympics. I think that's pretty amazing, and most people would agree.

Still, when Ms. Ederle decided to swim across the English Channel, everyone said it couldn't be done. It wasn't because she wasn't a good swimmer. Several men had already succeeded in swimming across the Channel from France to England. But it's a 21-mile swim! People said there was no way a woman could swim that far.

Gertrude Ederle proved them all wrong when, on August 6, 1926, she became the first woman in the entire world to swim across the English Channel. It took 14 hours and 31 minutes, but she did it. Hurray for girls! Not only that, but she did it two hours faster than any of the men who did it before her. So there!

Where Did You Go, Peppermint Patty and Marcie?

Flying the blue skies like Amelia Earhart!

"Adventure is worthwhile in itself."
—Amelia Earhart

Amelia Earhart wasn't the first woman to fly an airplane, but she was the first woman to fly over the Atlantic Ocean. She was also the first person (man or woman) to fly solo over the Pacific from Hawaii to California. Oh, and did we mention that she flew all by herself! Earhart's flight career took off in the early days of aviation. She became famous for her daring adventures. People loved reading about her in newspapers and in books that she wrote about her flights.

In 1937, Ms. Earhart set out to be the first woman pilot to circle the globe. She and her navigator, Fred Noonan, made stops in South America, Africa, India, Southeast Asia, and South America. When they left the island of New Guinea they just had 7,000 miles left to finish the flight. But they never made it to the next stop. No one knows for sure what happened, and it is still a mystery. Amelia Earhart is our hero, and we are glad she had the courage to take off and fly!

I WONDER IF NEIL ARMSTRONG MET THE MAN ON THE MOON?

Where Did You Go, Schroeder?

Moonwalking like Neil Armstrong!

"That's one small step for man, one giant leap for mankind."

—Neil Armstrong

Neil Armstrong had an out-of-this-world adventure. He made history as an astronaut in 1969 when he rocketed off from Earth on the spaceflight called Apollo 11. Mr. Armstrong was the commander, and the destination was—drum roll, please—the moon! The whole world breathed a big sigh of relief when the spacecraft successfully landed on the moon. Then they cheered when Neil Armstrong stepped out of the lunar module and became the first man in history to walk on the moon. Millions of people around the world watched it happen on live television.

Mr. Armstrong left an American flag and a plaque on the moon. The plaque said, HERE MEN FROM THE PLANET EARTH FIRST SET FOOT UPON THE MOON JULY 1969 A.D. WE CAME IN PEACE FOR ALL MANKIND.

Bravo, Neil Armstrong!

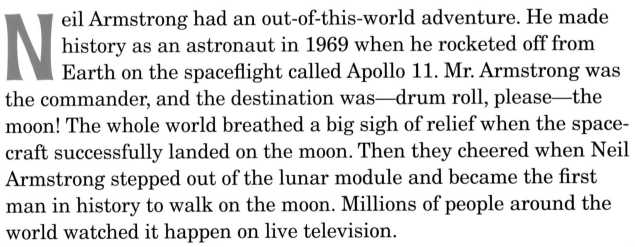

Where Did You Go, Reader?
Describe it!

If you were an explorer, where would you go?

(Woodstock says to make sure you use a separate piece of paper if this book doesn't belong to you.)

_____

_____

_____

_____

_____

_____

_____

_____

_____

_____

_____

_____

_____

_____

Where Did You Go, Reader?

Show it!

Draw a picture of your exploration adventure.

(Woodstock says to make sure you use a separate piece of paper if this book doesn't belong to you.)